Baboushka

For seekers of all ages, places and times
past, present and to come A.S.

For Laurence Pennant-Jones with much love H.C.

Baboushka

Retold by Arthur Scholey

Illustrations by Helen Cann

LION
Children's Books

All the villagers were out, bubbling with excitement.

'Did you see the star again last night?'

'Of course we did.'

'Much bigger.'

'It was moving, coming towards us. Tonight it will be high above us.'

That night, excitement, like a wind, scurried through the lanes and alleys.

'There's been a message.'

'An army is on the way.'

'Not an army – a procession.'

'Horses and camels and treasure.'

Now everyone was itching for news. No one could work. No one could stay indoors.

No one, that is, but Baboushka. Baboushka had work to do – she always had. She swept, polished, scoured and shined. Her house was the best kept, best polished, best washed and painted. Her garden was beautiful, her cooking superb.

'All this fuss for a star!' she muttered. 'I haven't time even to look. I'm so behind, I must work all night!'

So she missed the star at its most dazzling, high overhead. She missed the line of twinkling lights coming towards the village at dawn. She missed the sound of pipes and drums, the tinkling of bells getting louder. She missed the voices and whispers and then the sudden quiet of the villagers, and the footsteps coming up the path to her door. But the knocking! She couldn't miss that.

'Now what?' she demanded, opening the door.

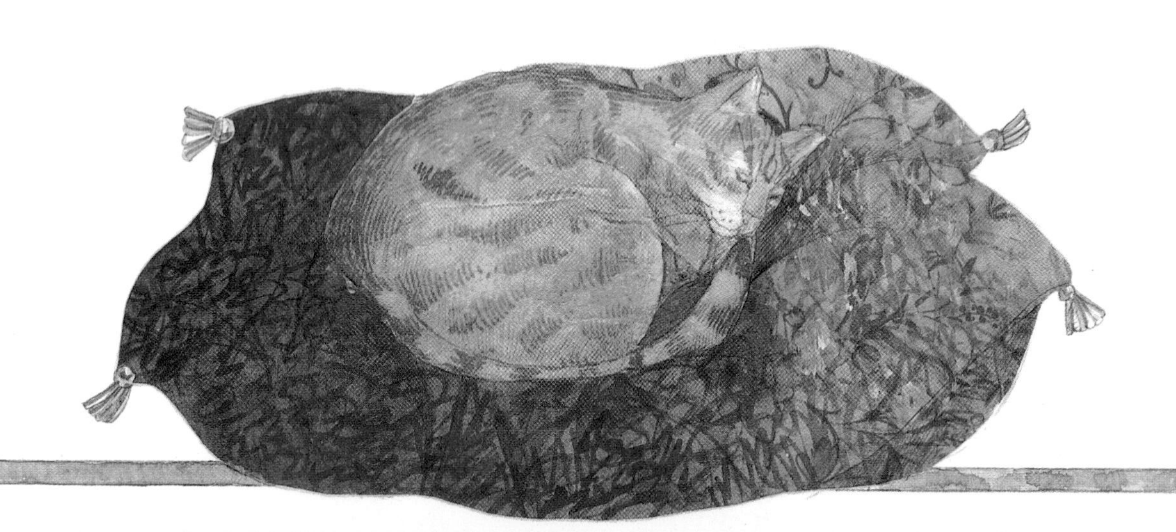

Baboushka gaped in astonishment.

There were three kings at her door!

'We seek a place to rest,' they said. 'Yours is the best house in the village.'

'You… want to stay here?'

'It would only be till night falls and the star appears again.'

Baboushka gulped. 'Come in, then,' she said.

How the kings' eyes sparkled at the sight of the feast Baboushka set before them.

As she dashed about, serving them, Baboushka asked question after question.

'Have you come a long way?'

'Very far,' sighed Caspar.

'And where are you going?'

'We're following the star,' said Melchior.

'But where?'

They didn't know, they told her. But they believed that it would lead them to a new-born king, a king such as the world had never seen before, a king of Earth and Heaven.

'Why don't you come with us?' said Balthasar. 'Bring him a gift as we do. See, I bring gold, and my friends bring spices and salves.'

'Oh,' said Baboushka. 'I am not sure that he would welcome me. And as for a gift…'

'Why, this pickle's fit for any king!' cried Balthasar.

Baboushka laughed. 'Pickle? For a baby? A baby needs toys.' She paused. 'I have a cupboard full of toys,' she said sadly. 'My baby son, my little king, died while very small.'

Balthasar stopped her when she next bustled by.

'This new king could be your king, too. Come with us when the star appears tonight,' he said.

'I'll… I'll think about it,' sighed Baboushka.

As the kings slept, Baboushka tidied as quietly as she could. What a lot of extra work there was! And this new king. What a strange idea – to go off with the kings to find him. Yet, could she possibly do it? Leave home and go looking for him just like that?

Baboushka shook herself. No time for dreaming! All this washing-up, and putting dishes away, and extra cooking. Anyway, how long would she be away? What would she wear? And what about gifts?

She sighed. 'There is so much to do. The house will have to be cleaned when they've gone. I couldn't just leave it.'

Suddenly, it was night-time again. There was the star!

'Are you ready, Baboushka?'

'I'll... I'll come tomorrow,' Baboushka called. 'I'll catch up. I must just tidy here, find a gift, get ready...'

The kings waved sadly. The star shone ahead. Baboushka ran back into the house, eager to get on with her work.

Sweeping, dusting, beating all the cushions and carpets, cleaning out the kitchen, cooking – away went the night.

At last she went to the small cupboard, opened the door and gazed sadly once again at all those toys. But how dusty they were! One thing was certain. They weren't fit for a baby king. They would all need to be cleaned.

Better get started at once.

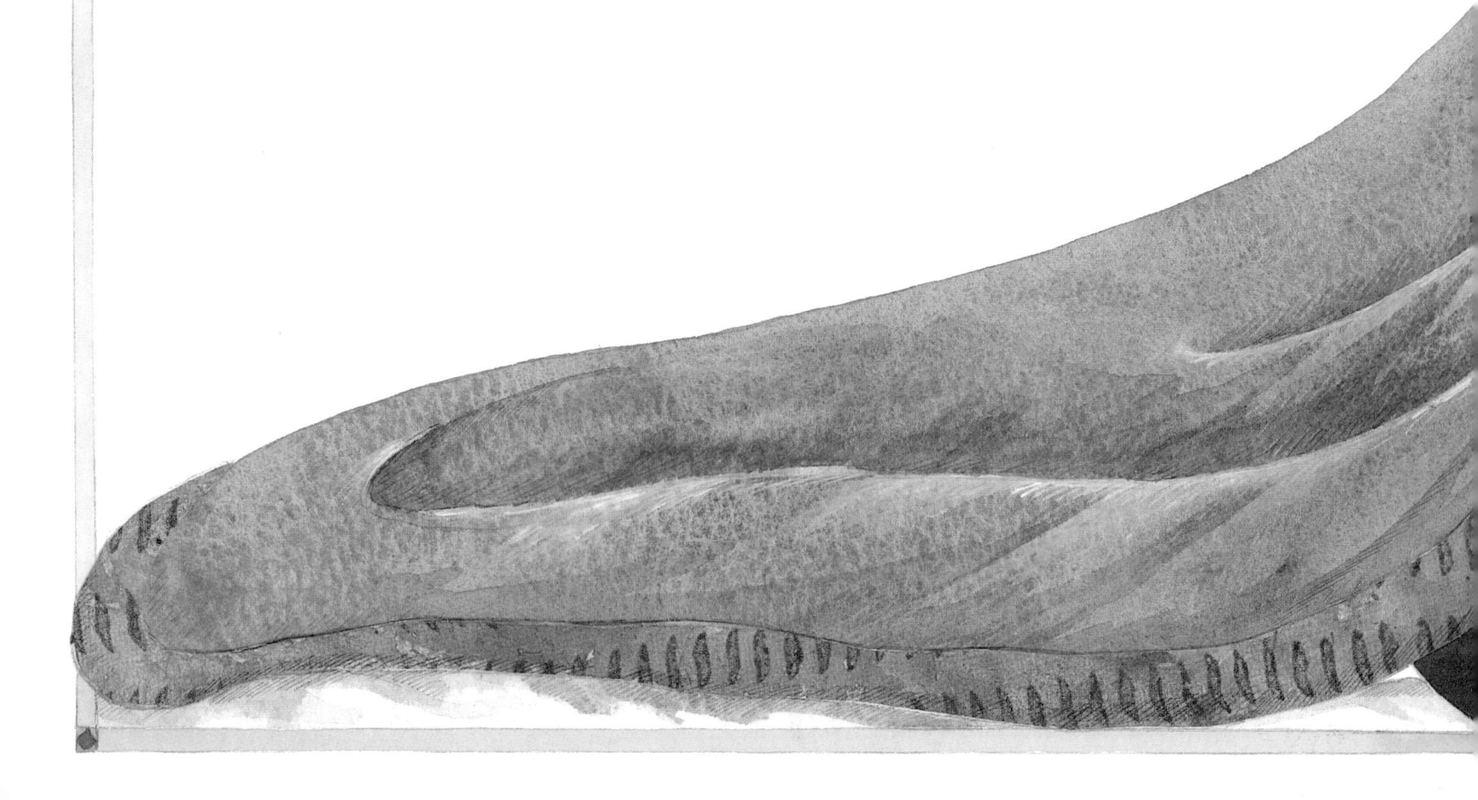

On, on, she worked. One by one, the toys glowed, glistened and gleamed. There! Now they were fit for the royal baby.

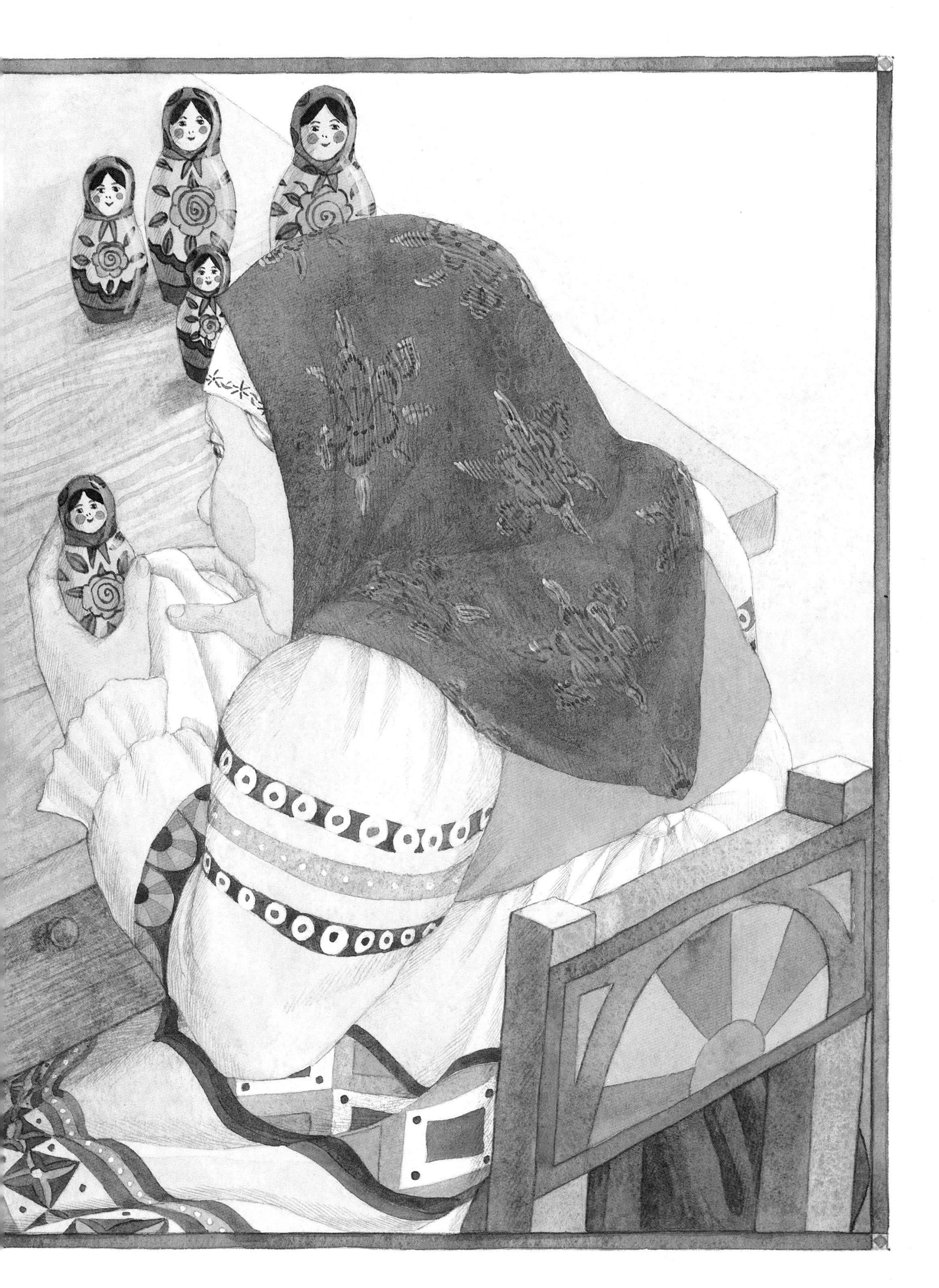

Baboushka looked through the windows. It was dawn! There was the sound of the farm cockerel. She looked up. The star had gone. The kings would have found somewhere else to rest by now. She would easily catch them up.

At the moment, though, she felt so tired. Surely she could rest now – just for an hour…

Suddenly, Baboushka was wide awake. It was dark. She had slept all day! She ran out into the street. No star. She rushed back into the house, pulled on her cloak, hurriedly packed the toys in a basket and stumbled down the path the kings had taken.

On she went, hurrying through village after village. Everywhere she asked after the kings.

'Oh yes,' they told her, 'we saw them. They went that way.'

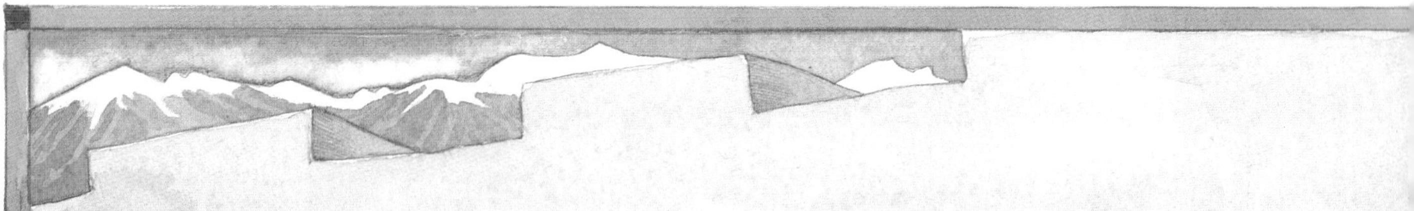

Baboushka lost count of the passing days. The villages grew bigger and became towns. But Baboushka never stopped, through night and day. Then she came to a city.

The palace! she thought. That's where the royal baby would be born.

'No royal baby here,' said the palace guard.

'Three kings? What about them?' asked Baboushka.

'Ah yes, they came. But they didn't stay long. They were soon on their way again.'

'But where to?'

'Bethlehem – I can't imagine why. It's a very poor place. But that's where they went.'

She set off at once.

It was evening when Baboushka wearily arrived at Bethlehem. How many days had she been on the journey? She could not remember. And could this really be the place for a royal baby? It didn't look like it. It was not much bigger than her own village. She went to the inn.

'Oh yes,' said the landlord, 'the kings were here two days ago. There was great excitement. But they didn't even stay the night.'

'And a baby?' Baboushka cried. 'Was there a baby?'

'Yes,' said the landlord, 'there was. Those kings asked to see the baby, too.'

When he saw the disappointment in Baboushka's eyes, he stopped.

'I'll show you where the baby was,' he said gently. 'I couldn't offer the poor couple anything better at the time. My inn was packed full. They had to stay in the stable.'

Baboushka followed him across the yard.

'Here's the stable,' he said. Then he left her.

'Baboushka?'

An angel was standing in the half-light of the doorway. He looked kindly at her. Perhaps he could tell her where the family had gone? Baboushka knew now that the baby king was the most important thing in the world to her.

'They have gone to Egypt, and safety,' he told Baboushka. 'And the kings have returned to their kingdoms. But one of them told me about you. I am sorry but, as you see, you are too late. Shepherds came as soon as the angels told them. The kings came as soon as they saw the star. It was Jesus the Christ-child they found, the world's Saviour.'

It is said that Baboushka is still looking for the Christ-child, for time means nothing in the search for things that are real. Year after year, she goes from house to house calling, 'Is he here? Is the Christ-child here?'

And at Christmas, when she sees a sleeping child and hears of good deeds, she will lift out a toy from her basket and leave it, just in case.

Then, on Baboushka goes with her journey, still searching, still calling, 'Is he here? Is the Christ-child here?'

The Baboushka Carol

Words: Arthur Scholey Music: Donald Swann

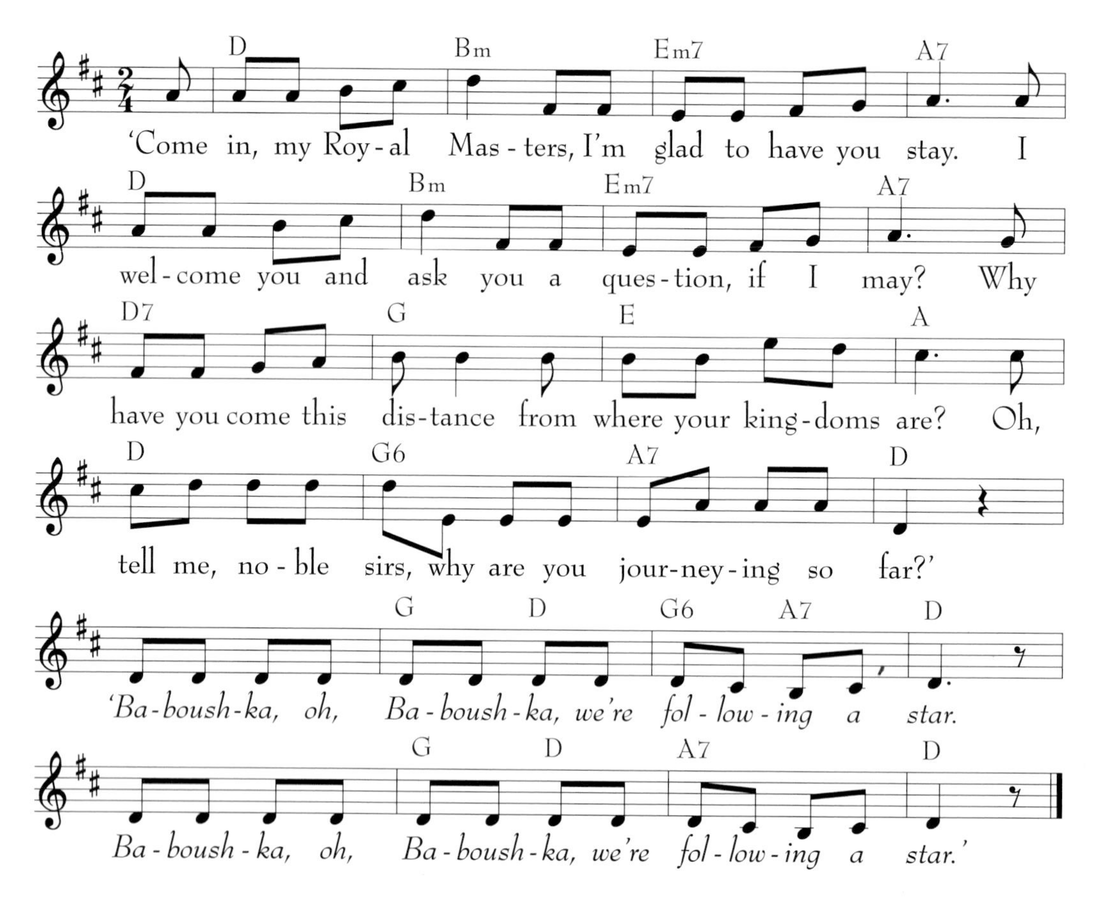

'The star's a mighty marvel,
A truly glorious sight.
But, Lords, you must stay longer –
Oh, won't you stay the night?
Do tell me why you hurry –
And here's another thing:
I marvel at the meaning of the precious gifts you bring.'
'Baboushka, oh, Baboushka, they're for a new-born king.
Baboushka, oh, Baboushka, they're for a new-born king.'

'Some king, to have such treasures,
A star to show his birth,
And you to do him the honour,
The greatest ones of earth –
And yet he is a baby,
A tiny man is he?
O Royal Ones, I wonder, then, if he will welcome me?'
'Baboushka, oh, Baboushka, oh, why not come and see?
Baboushka, oh, Baboushka, oh, why not come and see?'

'I will, my Royal Masters –
But not just now, I fear.
I'll follow on tomorrow
When I have finished here.
My home I must make tidy,
And sweep and polish, too,
And then some gifts I must prepare – I have so much to do!'
'Baboushka, oh, Baboushka, we dare not wait for you.
Baboushka, oh, Baboushka, we dare not wait for you.'

At last I make the journey –
No star to lead me on.
'Good people, can you tell me
The way the kings have gone?'
Some shepherds tell of angels
But now there is no sound.
The stable, it is empty, and the baby Egypt-bound.
'Baboushka, oh, Baboushka, we know where he is found.
Baboushka, oh, Baboushka, we know where he is found.'

Through all the years I seek him
I feel him very near.
'O people, do you know him?
Oh, tell me: Is he here?
In all the world I travel
But late I made my start.
Oh, tell me if you find him for I've searched in every part.'
'Baboushka, oh, Baboushka, we find him in our heart.
Baboushka, oh, Baboushka, we find him in our heart.'

A Lion Children's Book
an imprint of
Lion Hudson plc
Mayfield House, 256 Banbury Road,
Oxford OX2 7DH, England
www.lionhudson.com
ISBN 0 7459 4456 6

First edition 1982
Second edition 1989
Third edition (hardback) 2001
Third edition (paperback) 2002
3 5 7 9 10 8 6 4

Acknowledgments
'The Baboushka Carol': words copyright © 1977 Arthur Scholey;
music copyright © The Estate of Donald Swann 1977.
Music typeset by MSS Studios, Dolgellau, Gwynedd.

A catalogue record for this book is available
from the British Library

Typeset in 15/24 Bernhard Modern
Printed and bound in Singapore

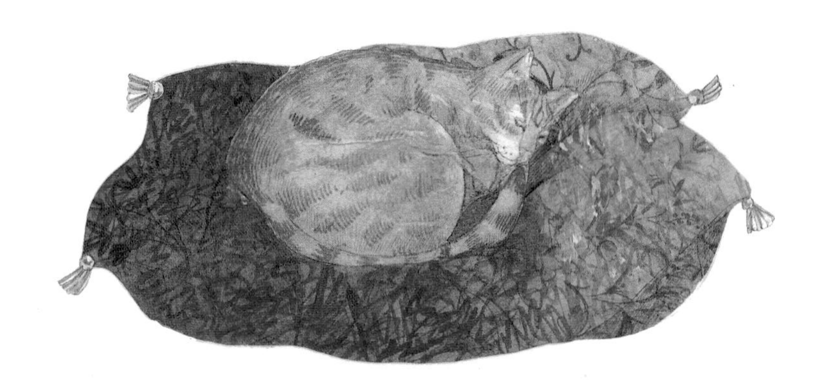